D0330706

TITLE MATERIALS

Library Media Center
Nancy Young Elementary School
800 Asbury Drive
Aurora, IL

Blackthorn's Changing Seasons

Based on the Original Flower Fairies™ Books
by Cicely Mary Barker

Frederick Warne

Every fairy in Flower Fairyland loves one season more than any other.

Some love spring or summer, when pretty petals open in the sun.

Others enjoy the ripe
fruits and golden
leaves of autumn.

Winter is magical
too, with sparkling
frosts and beautiful,
bare branches.

Blackthorn thinks she likes
early spring best of all.

"I love to feel the gentle sun on my
face," she smiles. "Spring makes
everyone happy!"

"It makes us want to dance!" her friends
the Crocus Fairies agree.

Day after day, more flowers open their petals and show their pretty faces to the sun. Soon Flower Fairyland is full of beautiful blossoms.

Gradually, spring is turning into summer.

"Perhaps summer is the best season after all," says Blackthorn.

Blackthorn loves to watch
the little fairies having fun
in the warm breeze.

Suddenly, she notices
something. Pretty white
petals are fluttering all
around her.

"Oh no!" she cries.
"Some of my flowers
are blowing away!
Come back!"

"Don't worry, Blackthorn!" says kind Forget-me-not. "Each season brings new surprises. You'll see."

Blackthorn is not so
sure. She looks at her
branches and sighs. It is
a long time before spring
will come again!

The weeks go by.
One warm summer's
evening, Blackthorn
watches sadly as
Willow dips her toes
in the stream.

"How lovely your
long, green leaves are,
Willow," she says.

"You have lovely
leaves, too, Blackthorn!"
laughs Willow.

Blackthorn is
surprised, but it is
true! Forget-me-not
was right. Everything
changes – even pretty
little fairies.

Autumn comes. Who is
this little fairy smiling
shyly amongst the leaves?
How pretty she looks!
It's Blackthorn!

She has a lovely new dress,
and her branches are full
of wild plums, called sloes.

"I am so happy that
autumn is here!" she cries.
"And I can't wait for
winter, too. Then my fruits
will be sweeter and ready
to eat."

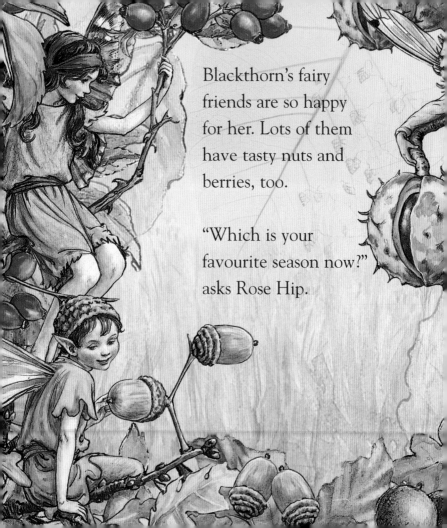

Blackthorn's fairy
friends are so happy
for her. Lots of them
have tasty nuts and
berries, too.

"Which is your
favourite season now?"
asks Rose Hip.

"All of them!" laughs Blackthorn. "It's lovely all year round in Flower Fairyland!"

FREDERICK WARNE
Published by the Penguin Group
Penguin Books Ltd, 80 Strand, London WC2R 0RL, England
New York, Australia, Canada, India, New Zealand, South Africa

This edition first published by Frederick Warne in 2005

3 5 7 9 10 8 6 4 2

Copyright © Frederick Warne and Co., 2005
New reproductions of Cicely Mary Barker's illustrations
copyright © The Estate of Cicely Mary Barker, 1990
Copyright in original illustrations
© The Estate of Cicely Mary Barker 1923, 1925, 1926,
1928, 1934, 1940, 1944, 1946, 1948
All rights reserved.

ISBN 0 7232 5378 1

Printed in China